Aviva Gittle Publishing
Kitten and Friends Series
Kitten & Snake

Written by Aviva Gittle
Illustrated by Tekla Huszár

Kitten & Snake

Book 4 of the Kitten and Friends series

Written by Aviva Gittle
Illustrated by Tekla Huszár

Page Layout
Sergei Bobryshev

Editors
Sara Dean
Carol Thompson
Milo Shapiro of IMPROVentures

ISBN: 1502886294
ISBN 13: 978-1502886293

CreateSpace Independent Publishing Platform
North Charleston, South Carolina

www.GittlePublishing.com

To my father, Alan Kibbe Gaynor, who
loves Kitten as much as I do.

The stick was moving in the air and hitting the rock. It looked just like the toy the human used to play with Kitten.

Kitten swatted it with his paw. But the stick got longer and moved along the grass in small curves.

"I wouldn't do that if I were you," said the stick.

"I didn't know sticks could talk," said Kitten.

"I'm not a stick. I'm a snake. And you just swatted my tail."

"My puppy friend lets me swat his tail," said Kitten.

"I'm a snake, not a puppy. If you weren't so fluffy and cute, I would swat you back," said Snake.

"But I wouldn't hurt you," said Kitten. "I just want to play."

"Snakes don't play with kittens," said Snake.

"Why not?" asked Kitten.

"They just don't," said Snake. He wrapped his long body into a ball and raised his head up high in the air.

"That's not a very good reason," said Kitten. "Why can't a snake play with a kitten?"

"What kind of game could a snake play with a kitten?"

As Snake talked his tongue slid out of his mouth and wiggled in the air. Swatting Snake's tongue looked as fun as swatting his tail. Kitten thought about it, but decided it might not be a good idea.

"What do you do all day?" asked Kitten.

"I eat, I sleep and I slither," said Snake.

"What's slither?" asked Kitten.

"I move around," said Snake. "Like this."
Snake lowered his head to the ground and
swung his body one way and then the other.
He looked like a thick piece of yarn.

"That looks hard," said Kitten.

"Why do you say that?" asked Snake.

"You have no legs. You have no paws!"

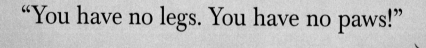

"I am very strong," said Snake. "I don't need legs and I don't need paws to help me move."

Kitten wondered what it would be like to move with no legs and no paws. He flopped on the ground, rolled on his back and wiggled around, but he didn't get very far.

"It's not working!" cried Kitten.

"You're not strong like a snake," said Snake. He continued to slither on the ground. "But it was a good try."

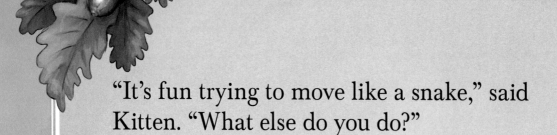

"It's fun trying to move like a snake," said Kitten. "What else do you do?"

"I molt," said Snake.

"How do you molt?" asked Kitten.

"I shed my skin," explained Snake.

"Is it just like when kittens shed their fur?"

"Sort of," said Snake, "but it's like shedding my whole body at once."

"Molting doesn't sound very fun," said Kitten.

"Hmm, you're right, it's not fun," said Snake. "It's just something I have to do."

Kitten liked talking to Snake, but he wanted to play.

What Kitten really wanted to do was swat Snake's tail some more. But he didn't want to make Snake mad. So he swatted a blade of grass that was swaying in the wind instead.

"There must be something we can do together," said Kitten. "Do you like to hide?"

"Yes! I hide all the time!" said Snake. He was starting to like the idea of playing a game with Kitten.

"We can play hide and seek," said Kitten.

"That sounds fun," said Snake. "What do you do?"

"I'll run over to the big oak tree and while I'm gone you hide."

"Then what?" asked Snake.

"I'll run back and try to find you!"

Snake found a lot of places to hide - in the tall grass, behind a rock, and in the pond. Kitten didn't know snakes could swim!

Snake was easy to find because his tail was always sticking out from his hiding place.

Kitten didn't tell Snake that he was easy to find. He didn't want to hurt his feelings.

They played all day until Kitten's human friend called out, "Kitten! Dinner time!"

"I hope we get to play again soon," said Snake. He was truly sad to see his new friend go.

"We will!" promised Kitten.

That night, Kitten drank a whole bowl of
milk. He thought about how much fun he
had playing hide and seek with his new
friend, Snake.

Then he jumped up on his human friend's
lap and went to sleep. Kitten dreamed that
Snake let him swat his tail ... just a little bit.

Moral of the Story

Someone may look mean and rough.
But they're really not so tough.
Give them a chance to be your friend.
They may surprise you in the end.

The End

Kitten is so happy that you stopped by to visit! Please show Kitten some love and leave a review on Amazon. Just search Amazon.com for "Aviva Gittle" to find this book and to see a list of all of Aviva's exciting stories for children.

Aviva Gittle Publishing
Kitten and Friends Series

Kitten & Snake
Coloring Book

Written by Aviva Gittle
Illustrated by Tekla Huszár

"I'm not a stick. I'm a snake. And you just swatted my tail."

"My puppy friend lets me swat his tail."

"What kind of game could a snake play with a kitten?"

"I eat, I sleep and I slither."

Kitten tries to slither like Snake.

Kitten really wanted to swat Snake's tail.

"I'll run back and try to find you!"

Snake was easy to find.

Kitten didn't know that snakes can swim.

Kitten dreams of his new friend Snake.

Aviva Gittle

Hi! My name is Aviva Gittle and I love to tell stories. I've been writing since I was a little girl. Long, long ago, I was born in New York. Now I live in San Diego, the most beautiful city in the world! In 2013, I decided to self-publish my first story, *Mort the Fly*. Since then, I have written many more stories including the 8-book series, *Kitten and Friends*, *In Nana's Arms* and *Bagel Boy*. I want to know more about you and learn your stories, too! So be sure to visit me at: www.GoToGittle.com.

Tekla Huszár

Hi! My name is Tekla Huszár, I'm from Hungary. As an artist, I sculpt, paint, and illustrate stories. Among all of these, illustrating children's books is my favorite. Being a mother, I really enjoy reading stories of every kind, immersing myself in the secret realm of a child's limitless imagination. I find great joy in creating the characters for the stories I'm asked to illustrate. Using my imagination to make them appear to others is such a pleasure. This is why I have loved bringing Kitten and all of his friends to life! To view my work, visit: www.facebook.com/HuszarTekla

More Great Stories
From Aviva Gittle Publishing

My First Chapter Books

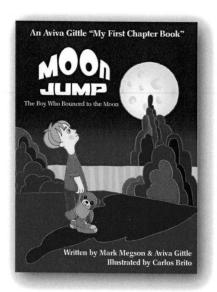

Other Books

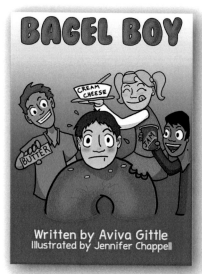

59106299R00024

Made in the USA
San Bernardino, CA
02 December 2017